FINDING Kindness

Deborah Underwood   illustrated by Irene Chan

Henry Holt and Company
New York

For Mom
—D. U.

To Xingpiao, Diana, and Doris,
for your kindness when I needed it most
—I. C.

Henry Holt and Company, *Publishers since 1866*
Henry Holt® is a registered trademark of Macmillan Publishing Group, LLC
120 Broadway, New York, NY 10271
mackids.com

ISBN 978-1-250-23789-7
Library of Congress Control Number 2019932415

Our books may be purchased in bulk for promotional, educational, or business use. Please contact your local bookseller or the
Macmillan Corporate and Premium Sales Department at (800) 221-7945 ext. 5442 or by email at MacmillanSpecialMarkets@macmillan.com.

First edition, 2019

Design by Mallory Grigg

Illustrations were done with watercolor on paper and retouched digitally in Photoshop. The kid's drawings on the card, in the beginning and the end of the
book, were created with crayons and oil pastels, respectively, by the artist's seven-year-old son, Connor Lai.

Printed in China by RR Donnelley Asia Printing Solutions Ltd., Dongguan City, Guangdong Province

10 9 8 7 6 5 4 3 2 1

Kindness is sometimes
a cup and a card

or a ladder,
a truck,
and a tree;

a scritch
and a cuddle,

a rake and a yard,

a cookie,

a carrot,

a key.

It's seeds and a feeder,

a seat on the train,

a daisy, a peach, or a pie;
a wave at a baker,
a boost on a crane,
a sandwich shared up in the sky.

Kindness is sometimes a tip in a case
or a tap when a lace is untied;

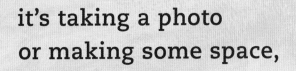

it's taking a photo
or making some space,

it's a racket,
a rocket, a ride.

It's dirt and a shovel,
petunias and pails,
it's trees that will someday give shade.

It's plans and a hammer,
it's lumber and nails,

it's houses and cold lemonade.

Kindness is sometimes just taking a break
or sitting with someone who's sad,

forgiving yourself when you've made a mistake
or forgiving a friend who got mad.

It's cuddling puppies,
it's holding a door,
it's a toy and a treat and a comb.

It's seeing the animals others ignore,
it's a leash and a lick and a home.

Kindness is sometimes a song or a stick
or a "Hi!" and a bat and a ball.

It's soup when a neighbor is sneezy and sick

or a scoop if one happens to fall.

It's reading a story,
it's feeding a fish,

it's a bucket,
a book,
and a yard.

It's kissing a sister,

it's a bug

and a cup

and a card.